Slinky Malinki

Lynley Dodd

PUFFIN BOOKS

Slinky Malinki
was blacker than black,
a stalking and lurking
adventurous cat.
He had bright yellow eyes,
a warbling wail
and a kink at the end
of his very long tail.

He was cheeky and cheerful,
friendly and fun,
he'd chase after leaves
and he'd roll in the sun.

But at night he was wicked
and fiendish and sly.
Through moonlight and shadow
he'd prowl and he'd pry.

He crept along fences,
he leaped over walls,
he poked into corners
and sneaked into halls.
What was he up to?
At night, to be brief,
Slinky Malinki
turned into a
THIEF.

All over town,
from basket and bowl,
he pilfered and pillaged,
he snitched and he stole.
Slippers and sausages,
biscuits, balloons,
brushes and bandages,
pencils and spoons.

He pulled them,
he dragged them,
he HEAVED them until...
he'd carried them home
to his house on the hill.

One rascally night
between midnight and four,
Slinky Malinki
stole MORE than before.
Some pegs and a teddy bear
dressed up in lace,
a gardening glove
from Macafferty's place.

A tatty old sneaker,
a smelly old sock
and Jennifer Turkington's
pottery smock.

A squishy banana,
some glue and a pen,
a cushion from
Oliver Tulliver's den.

A clock and some bottles,
a pair of blue jeans,
a half-knitted jersey,
a packet of beans.
He pulled them,
he dragged them,
he HEAVED them until...
he'd carried them home
to his house on the hill.

Then Slinky Malinki,
rapscallion cat,
piled them up high
in a heap on the mat.

The glue toppled over
and gummed up the pegs,
the jersey unravelled
and tangled his legs.
He tripped on the bottles
and slipped on the sock,
he tipped over sideways
and set off the clock.

CRASH went the bottles,
BEE-BEEP went the clock,
RO-RO-RO-RO
went the dogs on the block.
On went the lights,
BANG went the door
and out came the family,
one, two, three, four.

'Oh NO!' they all said,
'What a criminal cat!
Tomorrow we'll have to take
EVERYTHING back.'
With a tangled-up middle
and glue on his face,
Slinky Malinki
was deep in disgrace.

NEVER again
did he answer the call,
when moon shadows danced
over garden and wall.
When whispers of wickedness
stirred in his head,
he adjusted his whiskers
and stayed home
instead.